THE TERRIBLE BATTLE FOR BILLY WATSON

Clive Franks

ISBN-13: 978-1901679564 (First Century)
ISBN-10: 190167956X

First published in 1999 by Cromwell Publishers, Manchester
M22 0RR using the author name of Chip Walker.

For my wife Carol, and for School Teachers
everywhere who work hard to help our children

ACKNOWLEDGMENTS

With special thanks to Efecan Sezer
who in working to get this book published, assisted
greatly.

THE TERRIBLE BATTLE FOR BILLY WATSON

THE BEGINNING

It all started an awful long time ago, the war, you know. I've heard it said many times that there's never been a time before the war. Nobody knows how many have died, but we do know that it is many many millions, probably even trillions or zillions! Lots anyway.

The enemy just keep coming. We kill loads and manage to turn back many more, but still they come. I don't know how they get here, they're just here, all around us. We are forever under siege and surrounded.

The castle walls are thick and strong. For most of the time we are able to live a good and healthy life. Sometimes though, the invaders find a weakness, a way in. And when they do, there are terrible battles and many form both sides die.

There are many castles like ours. All are pretty much the same though they do come in a huge number of different sizes and even different colours. There are sad times when we hear that a castle has been overwhelmed or defeated. Sad because we know that all or many of those who lived there must have died. Dad says that we should never forget those who gave their lives but we should always remember that new castles are being born every day. He always says *'born'* but I think he really means *built*.

We know where the enemy comes from, yet nobody that I know has ever been there. It's a place far away called, 'Bacteria'. The horrible enemies from Bacteria have some really clever soldiers and fighters who use all sorts of tricks to get inside our castle. They call these the

Virus or the Germs,

Our castle has a strange name, but then again, all castles seem to have strange names. This one is called Billy Watson. Sometimes we just shorten it to Billy. I've never been outside, I don't think anyone has. No one has time, we are so busy patrolling our castle in case any of the virus or germs get in.

The invaders from Bacteria are always camped outside. They just wait for a door to open, or a part of the wall to break and then there's a mad scramble, a huge rush to get inside the walls of Billy Watson. Even if just one germ or virus survives, we can be hurt. You see they are not like us. I don't know how they do it, but one of them can somehow turn into two or three or even more.

Not very long ago when our castle was only eight years old there was a terrible battle, In a way it was an exciting time but also a frightening and a sad time, Millions died that day. I don't think any of us will ever forget it.

I remember it was a lovely sunny day

outside when in an instant and without any warning, Billy Watson tripped and banged a part we call his knee.

THE INVASION

The bang was so hard that it caused the castle wall to break. Someone said that it was cut right open and that some of our people who had been swimming in the blood canal were washed away and outside, never to be seen again.

As soon as the virus saw the opening one of their fiercest leaders let out a horrific yell and, urging his friends to follow, he shouted, "COME ON MEN! FOLLOW ME!" and "BILLY WATSON WILL SOON BE OURS!"

At that, hundreds of the viruses left their camp and rushed into the gash in Billy's knee. Immediately our gallant soldiers were fighting to stop the invaders but sadly most were quickly killed. When our Generals in the Headquarters, a place called the Brain, found out about the invasion, they sent our most special troops, the Antibodies.

The Antibodies fought valiantly but there were just too many invaders. Slowly, our people were pushed further back as the enemy took more and more control of Billy's body.

Somewhere outside, the enemy Generals heard of their victory and, spurred on by the good news, signaled to other troops and sent everything they had into the attack. They wanted to overwhelm and defeat Billy. All our defences were immediately put on high alert. This was going to be the fight of our lives!

Even during the fiercest battles we have to keep some of our castle doors open. Especially those that take in supplies such as; air, water and food. The enemy know that these, though heavily defended, remain the weakest points in our castle walls

That day, the Virus launched millions of invaders into the air. They flew frantically upon tiny specks of dust. They aimed their tiny aircraft to fly right down the throat of Billy Watson

As the virus entered the main door, or Billy's mouth as we like to call it, the Tonsil batteries went into action. Not every castle has Tonsils

but those that do like to use them for cleaning away unwanted visitors. The Tonsils stopped a lot if the invading flyers. They're good, but they're not that good, so quite a few of the bad guys managed to get in.

Once that the Generals in our brain found out what was happening, they quickly shut the door. Yet, already thousands of enemy germs and viruses were here and were looking for a way down Billy's throat. But within seconds, our clever defences went into action.

You see Billy's throat is covered in wet sticky stuff called Saliva. Many of the intruders became stuck there and couldn't break free. When the trapped flyers tried to wriggle away, Billy let out an almighty cough! And sent our enemies flying straight back out to where they had come from.

One or two of the germs and viruses, sitting astride their tiny craft continued down Billy's throat, zigzagging as they went. They avoided our traps of sticky saliva and loudly bellowed, " YEE HAH!" and "WE'VE GOT YOU NOW BILLY WATSON!"

What they didn't know was that deep down at the end of the throat tunnel is a place called the Stomach. Normally our stomach digests our food by pouring strong acid over it, breaking it down into pieces so small it can reach every part of our castle.

The flying viruses landed right into the darkest depths of our castle's stomach but luckily for us and before they could do any harm, they were quickly all killed off by the strong acid.

I've heard that the acid doesn't always kill all invaders and if this were to happen, then terrible illnesses can break out and our food becomes poisoned. Thankfully, because we are very careful with what we eat and drink, this hardly ever happens.
Other flying virus flew into Billy's nose!

The nose, though connected to the throat has rather different defences. You see just inside the nose are hundreds of little spikey hairs. These hairs are like barbed wire and not many specks of dust can get passed. When dust does become trapped in the hairs, the nose twitches and wiggles, itches and jiggles. This is a message to the brain so that the Generals can tell the lungs in the chest to blast a huge wave of air through the nose, pushing the dust and their pilots back outside. Sneezes are so powerful that when it happens, the whole castle can shake.

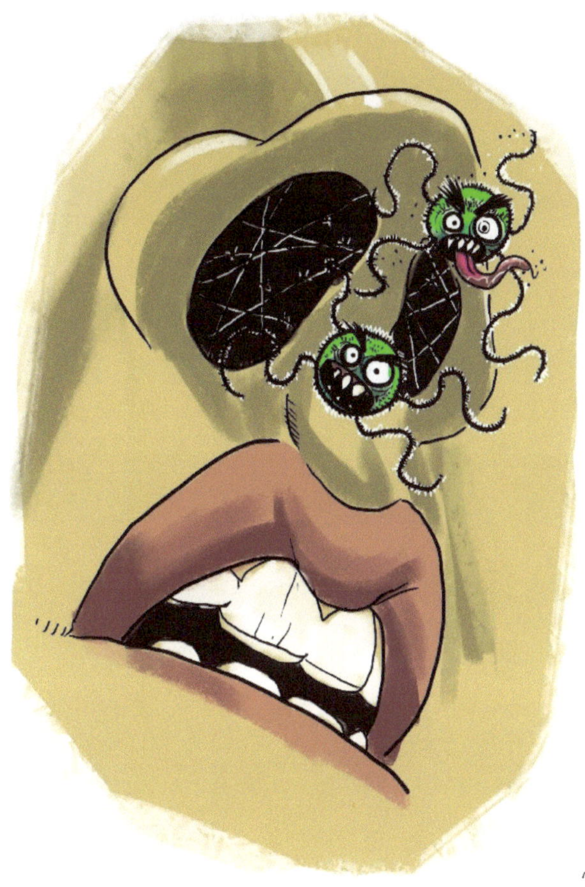

Outside, the enemy leaders became dismayed that their flying attack had failed so miserably. So they sent in their navy. The Bacteria navy had been waiting patiently in their tiny little ships of dirt hidden in the forest of hair on Billy's head.

THE FIGHT BACK

In the heat of a battle, Billy gets really hot and when that happens the castle sweats. Today was no different and the temperature inside Billy suddenly climbed to near boiling hot! And then there were torrents of water flooding down from the hair and heading straight towards Billy's eyes.

In those gurgling streams of sweat, the Bacteria swam and floated their way down aboard little ships, searching for a way in. Our castle, knowing that this could happen, built huge ridges of bone, flesh and hair. These are called eyebrows,

These ridges help divert the sweat away

from Billy's windows, his eyes. Even so, on this terrible day there was so much sweat that it breached the first fortifications and flooded onto the next line of defences.

Some sailors from Bacteria and a few Virus too, were clinging to Billy's eyes, gripping frantically, searching for a way in. Suddenly there was a look of terror on the faces of our enemies as a gigantic wall of skin and hair came crashing downward, brushing aside any unwanted dust and enemy.

This defence is most effective and it works really well. We call it blinking. I don't know how, but somehow we can do this loads of times.

On this day, luck was not with us. There were just too many virus soldiers. A few had managed to climb under and into our eyes.

Little did they know however, that whilst they were patting each other on their backs, congratulating themselves on how clever they had been, our Generals had ordered that our secret weapon should now be used. Abruptly and without any warning, Billy started to cry. Water gushed out from all the taps near our eyes, washing away even the most determined of nasty germs.

In other parts of the castle, Billy was not doing so well. Germs and Viruses from Bacteria had forced our fighters back. We were badly weakened. Some of our Generals thought that we might even lose the war. A decision was made that we should seek help from another place, somewhere outside the castle!

Everyone had heard about them, a strange but powerful army of killer robots, whose sole job is to hunt down and destroy germs and viruses. This army is very famous, they are known as the Medicine.

Urgent messages were sent outside calling the Medicine to us, then suddenly they arrived. Some came on a huge flying ship called, a Spoon, and they were quickly swallowed.

Some came in an injection, getting right into where the fighting was at its fiercest. Some even arrived on a sort of jelly called Lotion or Cream, sinking through tiny holes in the castle walls.

There are also pills and tablets, liquid drops, inhalers and even strange patches that work like lotions.

There are lots of ways that the robot army of Medicine can get in.

The Medicine are very powerful and because of this, everybody has to be very careful indeed. When I was very young, my

Dad told me about a castle called Samantha. Samantha had used the Medicine army even though they were not needed. You see, there just weren't any germs or virus inside that castle

The Medicine are good at killing enemy germs and viruses but if they come into a castle where there aren't any enemies, well, they can sometimes turn against us and some castles can become sick, This is exactly what happened to Samantha.

Once inside our castle, the Medicine army went straight into action, seeking out all the enemy germs and viruses.

Down near the knee, and the scene of the first battles, the robot army met the invading masses of germs and viruses. With our fighters at their side, the Medicine went forward, battling in tiny armoured vehicles. Our enemies didn't stand a chance

Within a few days all the nasty invaders had gone. Once that the Medicine had done their job, they just slowly disappeared.

Nowadays, I'm happy to tell you that Billy Watson is fit and healthy, but only because everyone in this castle works very hard to stay well. We all take great care with our food and drink and we are especially careful of who or what we allow inside our castle.

This is the way to be fit and healthy at all times.

ABOUT THE AUTHOR

Clive Franks was born in Croydon, Surrey, to Forces parents, and grew up in several countries including; Kenya, Singapore and Cyprus then returned to enlist into the British Army in 1975. He served for eleven years before joining the Police Service. Amongst his many and varied duties, he taught Drugs Education and Citizen Safety in schools. His first book, "The Terrible Battle for Billy Watson," was a local best seller and was nominated for several prestigious awards.

He has now written a number of adventure stories for children, all of which, aim to teach children that good shall always overcome evil.

THE TERRIBLE BATTLE FOR
BILLY WATSON

Also by Clive Franks;

Hadrian's Luck

PC Ted and the Secret Note

And in the name of Chip Walker;

Child of Hern

The Devil Wears Maroon

The Terrible Battle for Billy Watson